Mrs. Claus
Saves Christmas

(with the help of Mr. Mouse)

ISBN: 978-1-949752-00-7

Library of Congress Catalog Number: 2018910846
Printed in the United States of America
First Printing: 2018
22 21 20 19 18   5 4 3 2 1

Destination Wonder Press
PO Box 505
Laguna Beach, CA 92652

To order, visit www.destinationwonderpress.com or email us at requests@destinationwonderpress.com.

Davis – it's a privilege to share my business, life, and love with you. I could not have done this without you Boo!

To my children Kristen, Alex, Spenser and Slater – your love provides a constant source of joy and pride. I love to watch you grow and become the amazing people you are. Now you are all too old for the legend of Santa Claus. One day I hope to be reading the legend of Mrs. Claus to my grandchildren, and that long after I am gone, you will take it down off the shelf, dust it off and think of me when you are reading it to your children and your children's children.

To the reader . . .
I hope that you have at least half as much fun in the reading of this book as I've had in the writing.

Made with love,
Yvonne, Mom, aka M2

It was the night before Christmas and all through the house not a creature was stirring—not even Santa!!!

The stockings were hung by the chimney with hopes that Santa would soon be there,

but he knew with his flu, that if he flew,
all he would do is spread the flu…everywhere.

With Santa so sick, in bed was St. Nick!

He had to find someone to deliver the toys to all the good little girls and boys.

But who, oh who, could deliver the toys and deliver them with all his love enjoys?

He thought to himself about the children, all snug as bugs in their beds with sugar plum fairies dancing in their heads.

Santa thought maybe—though small as a baby, the lead elf could fly the reindeer this year.

Then he heard "I will do it!!" It was Mrs. Santa's voice. Oh, rejoice!

She popped into his room to check on the flu and to see what it was that she could do.

"Oh no!! You're sick with the flu and this, Papa Santa, this just won't do!

"I will be Santa this year!! I've got all the gear; there's nothing to fear. I can steer the Christmas reindeer!

"So off I go to lead the cheer and get the presents ready for the Christmas reindeer.

"With cocoa in hand, I'll set up a plan to give the children all that I can.

"Now go back to bed and ease your head. The elves and I will spread the cheer this year my dear!"

Mrs. Santa cried, "Dancer, Prancer, Comet, Cupid! Where's Rudolph? We need him ready and suited!" Snug in his bed. "Get up!" she said. "I need you to fly the sleigh tonight and Rudolph we need your nose to be bright!"

They sprang from their stalls ready to fly and help guide Mrs. Santa through the night sky.

Out in the snow in the North Pole, all the reindeer were ready to go, and set with a plan, to deliver they can, to every far-flung family and clan.

So off she flew without a care in sight. She knew this would be fun and oh what a night!

The moon and the stars glistened on the snow and the towns below had such a pretty glow. Struck by their beauty, she thought to herself, "What a pleasant surprise, the starry skies and the lovely light"—she knew why Santa did this every Christmas Eve night.

She knew in that moment the reindeer were lively and quick. She asked them for an extra kick: "Now Dasher, now Dancer, now Prancer, on Vixen, on Comet, on Cupid, on Donner and Blitzen—let's deliver the presents, lickety split!!!"

Rooftop to rooftop they flew through the night and kept out of sight with a sleigh full of toys. Mountaintops to seashores and all over the land delivering toys to all the little girls and boys. She filled their stocking and all their hopes and joys....

Happy as can be and filled with glee, she could see what a success this night would be. From now on, she thought, "We both will share and Christmas Eve will be a Claus affair!"

As the night came to a close and the sun started to rise, town folk rose from their doze and rubbed tired eyes. In the last little town, to all their wonder, a giggle was heard as loud as thunder. And as they looked up, at the break of day, they saw Mrs. Santa climb into her sleigh.

Not a word was spoken and to their surprise, she gave them a smile and waved her goodbyes!

. . . and a peep could be heard all through Santa's house, "Merry Christmas to all!" cried merry Mr. Mouse!

The End

 ## Yvonne Lane Wonder

Yvonne is a mom, author and entrepreneur, most recently the founder of Destination Sitters, LLC, a national hotel and event babysitting agency. Yvonne believes that the best way to teach a child is leading by example, with love, honesty, integrity, compassion, perseverance, and personal responsibility. Learning these values and teaching children that all women and men are equal will encourage them to dream big to be anything they want to be, even Santa!

CPSIA information can be obtained
at www.ICGtesting.com
Printed in the USA
LVHW010555170623
750059LV00015B/429